Good Things Come on Tiny Wings: The Adventures of Petalwink the Fairy®

Petalwink
Learns to Fly

by Angela Sage Larsen

For Aunt Gail:
who taught us to love and to read
and to love to read!

RISING STAR
STUDIOS
MINNEAPOLIS, MN

For other great resources contact Rising Star Education
888-900-4090
www.risingstareducation.com

Petalwink Learns to Fly
By Angela Sage Larsen

Text and Illustrations by Angela Sage Larsen

© 2006, 2010 Three Trees, Inc.
Three Trees, Inc. P.O. Box 92 Cottleville, MO 63338
1-877-70-PWINK
www.Petalwink.com™

Published in Minneapolis, MN by Rising Star Studios, LLC.

Printed in China:
Shenzhen Donnelley Printing Co., Ltd
Shenzhen, Guangdong Province, China
Completed: February 2010
P1_0210

Publisher's Cataloging-In-Publication Data
(Prepared by The Donohue Group, Inc.)

Larsen, Angela Sage.
    Petalwink learns to fly / by Angela Sage Larsen.

        p. : col. ill. ; cm. -- (Petalwink)

    Originally published in 2006 by Three Trees, Inc.
    Summary: Petalwink is aided by her well-meaning forest friends as she struggles to learn to fly.
    Interest age level: 002-009.
    ISBN: 978-1-936086-20-7 (hardcover/library binding)
    ISBN: 978-1-936086-34-4 (pbk.)

1. Flight--Juvenile fiction. 2. Fairies--Juvenile fiction. 3. Self-acceptance--Juvenile fiction.
4. Self-confidence--Juvenile fiction. 5. Flight--Fiction. 6. Fairies--Fiction.
7. Self-acceptance --Fiction. 8. Self-confidence--Fiction. I. Title.

PZ7.L278 Pd 2010
[E]   2009942879

Petalwink is a young fairy
whose time had come
to stretch her gossamer wings
and feel them hum.
Like you learned to walk, fairies learn to fly,
they float on the breeze and reach for the sky.

1

Newman Forest was aflutter one day.
Petalwink watched while her fairy friends made airplay:
Felicia's lavender wings like a butterfly queen
carried her through valleys, hills and places in-between;
the twins, Willow and Whitney, raced the air currents;
and June Bug balanced the breeze with perfect assurance.

Inspired by her friends
    and the hummingbirds hovering mid-air,
Petalwink sighed, "I wish, how I wish
    I could meet them up there."

Dazzled by lightning bugs
that lit up the night,
she longed to join them,
rise up and
take flight.

Gazing at noon
at the soaring bald eagle,
Petalwink hoped that
she'd soon be so regal.

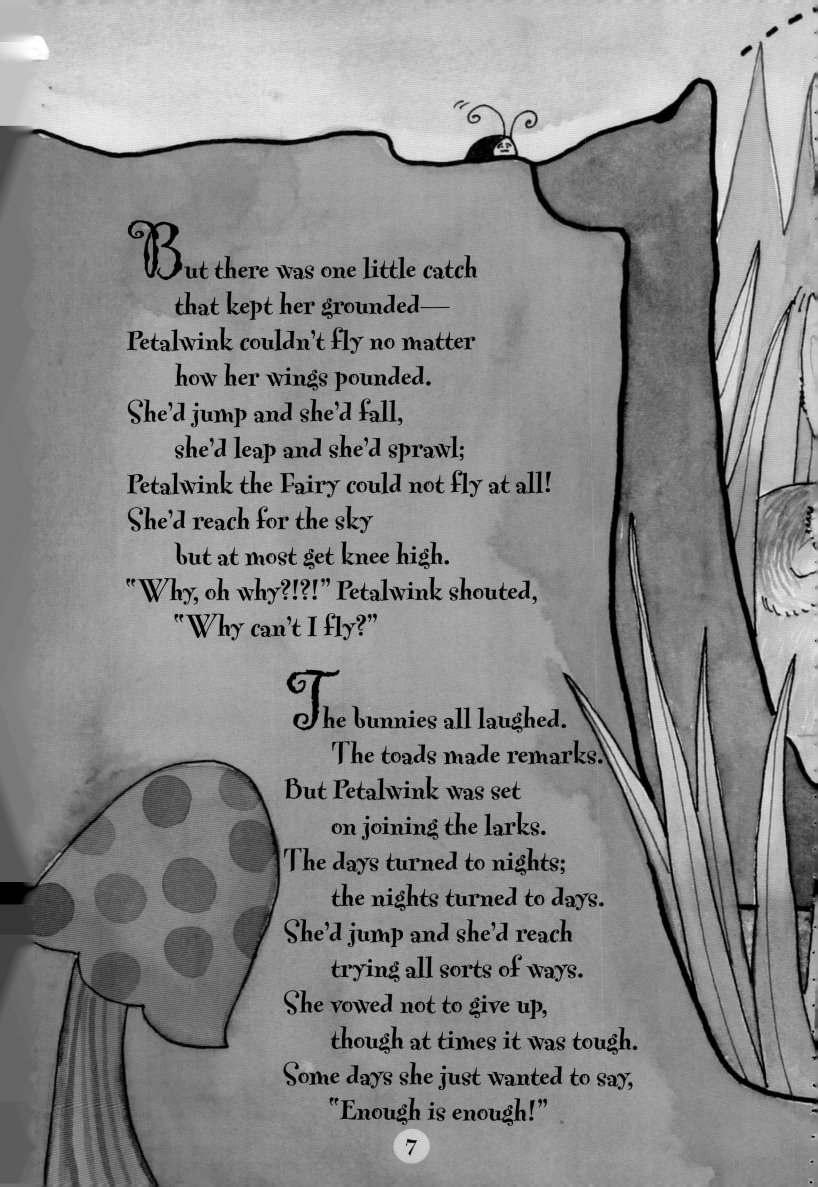

But there was one little catch
    that kept her grounded—
Petalwink couldn't fly no matter
    how her wings pounded.
She'd jump and she'd fall,
    she'd leap and she'd sprawl;
Petalwink the Fairy could not fly at all!
She'd reach for the sky
    but at most get knee high.
"Why, oh why?!?!" Petalwink shouted,
    "Why can't I fly?"

The bunnies all laughed.
    The toads made remarks.
But Petalwink was set
    on joining the larks.
The days turned to nights;
    the nights turned to days.
She'd jump and she'd reach
    trying all sorts of ways.
She vowed not to give up,
    though at times it was tough.
Some days she just wanted to say,
    "Enough is enough!"

7

Adrift on a lily pad,
    Petalwink pondered her plight.
Harry Bass swam beneath
    and noticed the sprite.
He sensed that his friend
    was lost deep in thought.
He wondered about her—
    she seemed so distraught.

He gurgled, "Hello!"
and asked how she fared.
Petalwink replied sadly,
"I am flying-impaired."

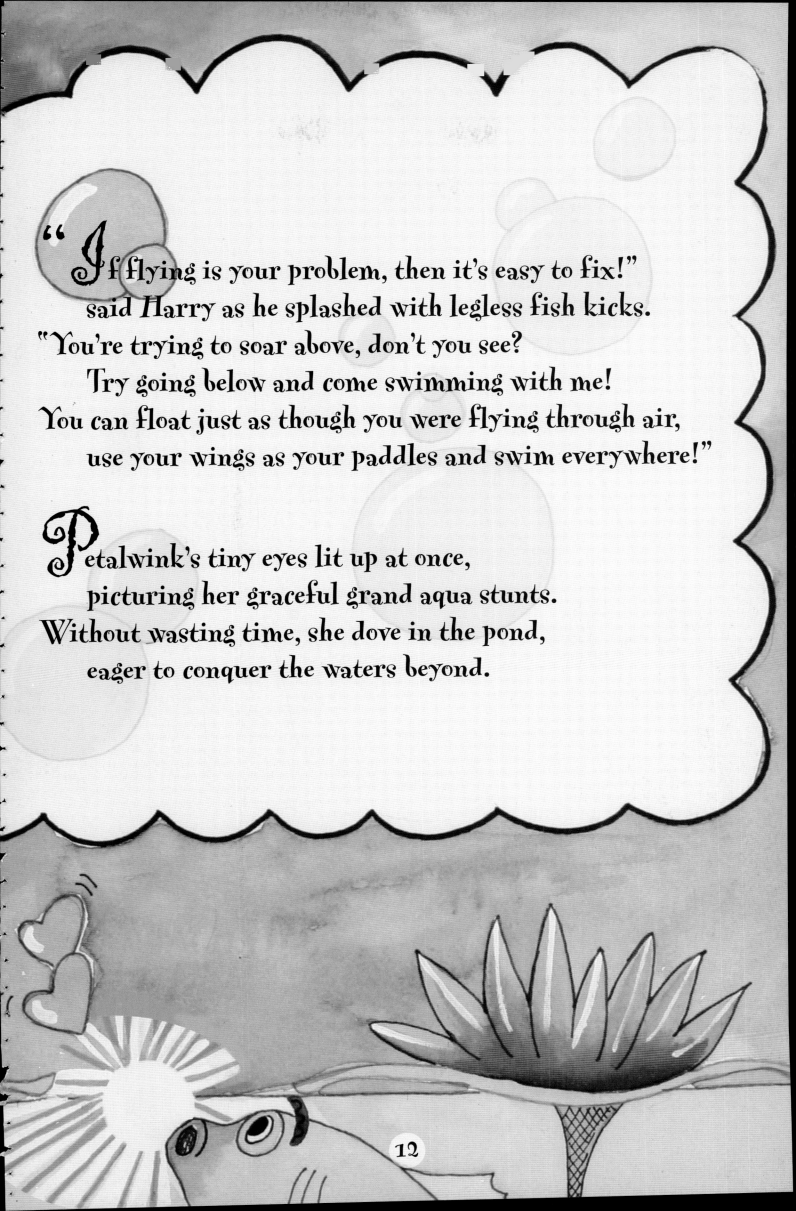

"If flying is your problem, then it's easy to fix!"
said Harry as he splashed with legless fish kicks.
"You're trying to soar above, don't you see?
Try going below and come swimming with me!
You can float just as though you were flying through air,
use your wings as your paddles and swim everywhere!"

Petalwink's tiny eyes lit up at once,
picturing her graceful grand aqua stunts.
Without wasting time, she dove in the pond,
eager to conquer the waters beyond.

The fish swam swiftly with a flick of his tail,
his gills helped him breathe, his fin was a sail.
Petalwink's wings, though, weren't strong enough;
she also discovered that breathing was tough.
Her journey ended quickly,
         she could still see the land
         as she broke through the surface,
         wheezing, "This did not go as planned!"
She gulped up the air, no mermaid she,
"I'm destined to live on the land—not in the sea."

She bid farewell
to Harry
and bobbed
to the shore,
still gasping fresh air,
using her wand as an oar.

She tottered out of the water, never so glad to see dirt.
She wrung out her wings and smoothed out her skirt.
She made her way past the cattails and grassy green weeds
and spied on Francis Frog jumping through the tall reeds.

An idea took hold as Petalwink spotted her friend,
"Francis has a webbed foot I'm sure he would lend!"

She still saw a way
     to get by without flight—
Francis could help, and (if she asked nicely)
     he just might.
"Hello Petalwink, may I offer you a snack?
     I have yummy bugs, fresh flies
     and scrumptious sumac!"

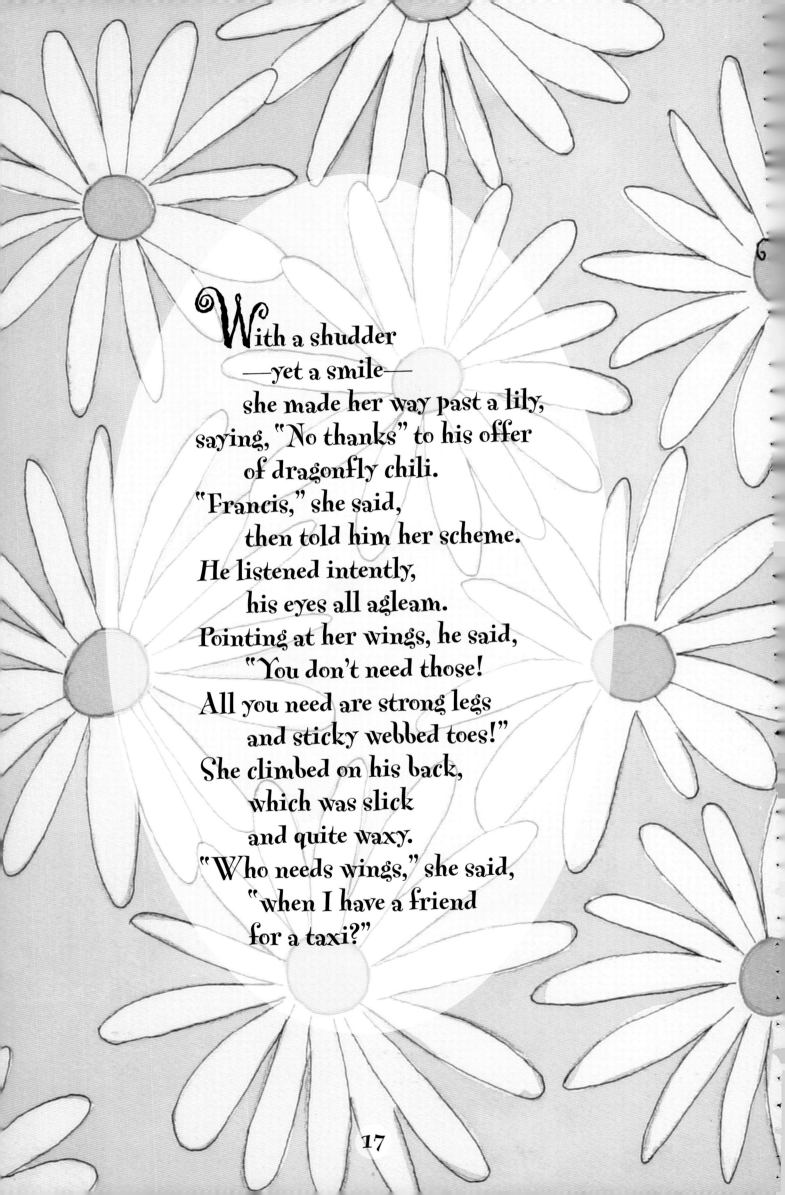

With a shudder
—yet a smile—
she made her way past a lily,
saying, "No thanks" to his offer
of dragonfly chili.
"Francis," she said,
then told him her scheme.
He listened intently,
his eyes all agleam.
Pointing at her wings, he said,
"You don't need those!
All you need are strong legs
and sticky webbed toes!"
She climbed on his back,
which was slick
and quite waxy.
"Who needs wings," she said,
"when I have a friend
for a taxi?"

At once they were off,
galloping webbed foot over foot,
but things shook loose on the fairy
that should have stayed put.

19

And before she knew it,
she flipped like a leaf in the breeze,
swinging off his back like off a trapeze.
Petalwink lay in the mud and said her goodbyes.
Francis kept hopping, distracted by flies.

Just then her pal Bliss Squiggle slithered by,
glistening in the sun like a silken necktie.
He saluted "hello" with a shake of his tail,
as he crossed paths with a leisurely snail.
"The key," she thought, "is to slip like a snake—
Bliss moves so smoothly
with a shimmy and a shake."

So Petalwink flopped
down onto her belly;
her shoulders went limp and her knees went to jelly.
But she couldn't budge, much less move,
her mouth filled with dirt—she was stuck in a groove.
"Maybe for being a snail I'd have a knack,
crawling along with a house on my back?"
But crawling was even slower than walking . . .
and with each new trial,
something in her was balking.

She stood up then and wiped
the dust off instead,
and she took a deep breath
to clear her wee head.
"So I don't have feathers,
fins or frog legs!
So I don't have scales,
a hard shell or lay eggs!"
Still, a lot about Petalwink
at that moment felt right—
"After all, my eyes twinkle,
my heart glows and
my smile is bright!"
Petalwink flung open her arms
for the whole world to see
and shouted out
as loud as she could,

"I'm glad to be me!"

Then with a quiver, a lilt,
and a little help from the breeze,
Petalwink lifted herself up
and soared through the trees!
"I can fly!" she squealed as she darted about.
"And I'm glad to be me!" she continued to shout.
So let the bunnies laugh.
Let the toads do their thing.
You too can soar when
you let your heart sing!

27

The next time you're out,
look up,
but don't blink.
You may see flying fairies,
and yes . . .
even Petalwink!

Visit Petalwink.com to learn
more about Petalwink and her friends,
play games, sign up to be a Petalwink
Pal by taking the Petalwink Pledge,
and find out what Petalwink has been
up to lately!

And . . . be on the lookout for
Petalwink Comes in Second, the second
storybook in the series, **Good Things
Come on Tiny Wings: The Adventures
of Petalwink the Fairy**®

Petalwink & You...

**Sometimes nothing feels better
than a good think.
So take a moment now to think Petalwink!**

♥ Why did Petalwink get so frustrated at the beginning of the story?

♥ Have you ever felt that way? What happened?

♥ What made you feel better?

♥ What made Petalwink feel better?

♥ What are her special talents?

♥ What are your special talents?

♥ Why didn't Petalwink give up?

♥ What would have happened to Petalwink if she had given up?

♥ What was something new that you learned how to do today?

Photo by: Michele Lugaro

Angela & Whit Larsen
Author/Illustrator & Business Manager

Angela is a professional artist and designer as well as the founder of two painting and mural businesses, A. Sage Designs and A.L.L. or nothin'. With her husband Whit, she opened an art gallery in Healdsburg, California. Soon after a periwinkle-haired fairy began visiting scraps of blank paper in Angela's studio and whispering her story in Angela's ear, Whit and Angela moved to their current home in O'Fallon, Missouri. There they formed Three Trees, Inc. to bring their signature character, Petalwink the Fairy® to life. The two continue to work on the rest of the books in the Petalwink storybook series.

Petalwink the Fairy® is the first character to be launched by Three Trees, Inc. Inspired by friends, cousins, and nieces, Petalwink was created to spread the time-less messages of kindness, courage, adventure and self-worth. Besides the children's books, the Petalwink the Fairy® brand will include stationery and gift items, home furnishings and decor, games and entertainment.

For more information, visit www.Petalwink.com